When it Snows

Richard Collingridge

When it snows . . .

all the cars are stuck and
the train has disappeared.

So, I follow the footprints

until I find a new way
to get around.

I play for the rest of the way

to the place where
the snowmen live.

And when the sun sinks,
I follow a bright light into the dark.

It leads me through the
gloomy forest

where I meet the
Queen of the Poles.

She takes me to a secret place

with tiny fairies that glow.

I see thousands
of elves

and a giant
reindeer
as well.

And I can go there
every day . . .

because my favourite
book takes me there.

THE END

dedicated to
Kim and Françoise